MRS. TOGGLE'S
CLASS PICTURE DAY

Story by Robin Pulver • Pictures by R.W. Alley

SCHOLASTIC INC.

Cartwheel BOOKS®

New York Toronto London Auckland Sydney Mexico City New Delhi Hong Kong

In loving memory of my dad, who didn't have to worry about bad hair days.
And for Antonio, our best hair fixer-upper.
—R.P.

For Robin, with thanks
—R.W.A.

ISBN 0-590-11741-6

Text copyright © 2000 by Robin Pulver.
Illustrations copyright © 2000 by R.W. Alley.
All rights reserved. Published by Scholastic Inc. SCHOLASTIC, CARTWHEEL BOOKS and associated logos are trademarks and/or registered trademarks of Scholastic Inc.

Library of Congress Cataloging-in-Publication Data

Pulver, Robin
Mrs. Toggle's class picture day / story by Robin Pulver; pictures by R.W. Alley.
      p. cm.
    "Cartwheel books."
    Summary: When Mrs. Toggle's bad hair day coincides with class picture day, her students, the custodian, the nurse, the art teacher, the librarian, and the principal all try to improve the situation.
    ISBN 0-590-11741-6 (pbk.)
    [1. Hair—Fiction. 2. Schools—Fiction.] I. Alley, R. W. (Robert W.), ill. II. Title.

PZ7.P97325 Mqp 2000
[E]—dc21   99-058609

10 9 8 7 6 5 4 3   00 01 02 03 04 05
                    Printed in the U.S.A.   24

First printing, October 2000

Go to www.scholastic.com for web site information
on Scholastic authors and illustrators.

As soon as Mrs. Toggle's children walked into their classroom in the morning, they ran right back out.

"Yikes!" yelled Joey.

"What was THAT?" cried Caroline.

The creature in their room came after them.

"Children! It's me, your teacher, Mrs. Toggle!
I'm having a bad hair day."

The children lowered their hands from their faces.

"It's Mrs. Toggle, all right," said Nina.

"But we shouldn't stare," said Caroline.

"Bad hair day?" said Joey. "It's more like a bad scare day!"

"I thought it was a nightmare day!" agreed Dina.

Paul said, "It will be a nightmare if we can't review subtraction for our test."

"Uh-oh," said Caroline.
"It's school picture day!"
"That's right," said Mrs. Toggle.
"I can't have my picture taken looking
like this!"

"Maybe we can help," said Caroline.
"It's worth a try," said Mrs. Toggle.

The children used paper clips and rubber bands on Mrs. Toggle's hair. They patted and sprayed and taped. They glittered and glued.

But when they were done, Mrs. Toggle's hair was still bad.

The principal, Mr. Stickler, stepped in. "Mrs. Toggle, is that you?" he asked. "What was all the shouting about?"

"I'm sorry, Mr. Stickler," said Mrs. Toggle. "The noise was my fault. I scared the children. I'm having a bad hair day."

"I have never heard of such a thing," said the principal. "But if your hair is being bad, you must bring it to my office for 'time out'. You come, too. I suppose your hair is attached to you."

"We're attached to Mrs. Toggle, too," said Caroline. "We love our teacher even when she's scary."

"Besides," said Paul, "we need to review subtraction for our test."

So Mrs. Toggle's hair headed for the principal's office. Mrs. Toggle went along with it, and so did Mrs. Toggle's students.

Mrs. Toggle sat down with her hair in the 'time out' chair.

But Mrs. Toggle's hair didn't stop being bad. It didn't settle down one bit.

"Oh, dear," said Mrs. Toggle. "Now I'm having a bad chair day as well as a bad hair day!"

The custodian, Mr. Abel, walked in. "Mrs. Toggle," he said, "is that you? Your hair! It looks…um…er…it looks just…um…great!"

"There's no need to be polite, Mr. Abel," said Mrs. Toggle. "I'm having a bad hair day."

"Hey, Mr. Abel!" said Dina. "You can fix everything! Could you repair Mrs. Toggle's hair?"

"Oh, yes, please!" begged Paul. "So we can get busy reviewing subtraction for our test."

"And so she'll look good for school pictures," said Nina.

Mr. Abel scratched his head. "I use a blow-dryer to fix my own hair, but there are no blow-dryers at school. I'll try to think of something else. Meanwhile, Mrs. Toggle, why don't you go see the nurse? When I have a bad back, I take medicine. Maybe Mrs. Schott has medicine for bad hair."

So Mr. Stickler gave Mrs. Toggle permission to take her hair to the nurse's office.

"I'm glad I never have bad hair," he said.

"You don't have much hair at all!" declared Caroline.

"It's been subtracted from your head," observed Paul.

"That's right," said Mr. Stickler. "My head is perfect. Perfect heads don't need hair to cover them up."

At the nurse's office, Mrs. Schott took one look at Mrs. Toggle and shrieked. "Mrs. Toggle, what bad hair you have!"

"I know," said Mrs. Toggle. "We're hoping you have medicine for it."

"To make it settle down," explained Nina.

"Like Mr. Abel's bad back, sometimes," added Dina.

Mrs. Schott shook her head.
"I have no medicine for bad hair, but
just in case bad hair is catching, you
had better wear a mask."

Mrs. Schott put a mask
over Mrs. Toggle's mouth and
nose to keep bad hair germs
from spreading.

"How can she teach subtraction with her mouth covered like that?" asked Paul.

"I will look ridiculous for school pictures," muttered Mrs. Toggle.

"It's the best I can do," said Mrs. Schott. "But why don't you go to the art room? Maybe Ms. Doodle can help you."

The art teacher, Ms. Doodle, was hanging finger paintings up to dry.

"Mrs. Toggle!" exclaimed Ms. Doodle. "It's not your day for art, is it? And WHAT in the world have you done to your hair?"

"She's having a bad hair day," explained Nina.

"We thought you could make her more beautiful for school pictures," said Dina.

"This is great!" exclaimed Ms. Doodle. "I will use my imagination! But, Mrs. Toggle, why are you wearing that ugly mask?"

"So she won't spread bad hair germs," said Dina, "if bad hair is catching."

"Oh," said Ms. Doodle. "I can make the mask look better, too." She painted polka dots on it. Then she said, "And now, for my masterpiece!"

Ms. Doodle fluffed and flipped and pushed and poufed. She added color here, color there, lots of color everywhere.

"There!" she said at last. "Children, how did I do?"

"Ms. Doodle," said Nina, "we don't want to hurt your feelings, but . . ."

"Our teacher's hair is still bad!" said Caroline.

"It's worse than ever!" blurted out Joey.

"Well!" said Ms. Doodle. "Some people don't appreciate fine art when they see it."

"Mrs. Toggle," suggested Dina. "Let's take your hair to the library. Maybe it would settle down for a story."

The children asked the librarian, Mr. Paige, to read them a story.

"A quiet story," explained Caroline, "is good for calming down wild things."

"Namely Mrs. Toggle's hair," said Joey.

"You've come to the right place," said Mr. Paige. He chose a book and began to read. His voice was calm and quiet, soft and soothing. Soon Mrs. Toggle and her class were sprawled on the floor, sound asleep.

When they woke up, Mrs. Toggle's hair was smushed on one side and standing up on the other.

Mrs. Toggle yawned. "You read that beautifully, Mr. Paige. But my hair is still bad!"

"Uh-oh," said Caroline. "It's time for school pictures."

Mrs. Toggle and her class headed for the auditorium.

"Oh, where is Mr. Abel with that blow-dryer?" asked Mrs. Toggle.

"There he is!" said Nina. "He doesn't have a blow-dryer. He has a . . ."

"Fan!" shouted everybody.

Suddenly, everybody's hair was bad,
except for Mr. Stickler's.

"Sorry, Mrs. Toggle," said Mr. Abel. "I guess that was too much air for your bad hair."

"That's quite all right, Mr. Abel," exclaimed Mrs. Toggle. "In fact, I'm forever grateful. Now I'm not the only one with bad hair!"

A few weeks later, when
the pictures were ready, Mrs. Schott
took one look and shouted,
"I was afraid bad hair was catching!"

Paul put his picture up
on his refrigerator at home.
"Who cares about bad hair,"
he said. "At least I passed
subtraction!"